D0884181

Professor Calculus

by Michael Farr

EGMONT

EGMONT
We bring stories to life

First published in Great Britain in 2007
by Egmont UK Limited
239 Kensington High Street, London W8 6SA

Originally designed and published by Éditions Moulinsart

ISBN 978 1 4052 3062 9

1 3 5 7 9 10 8 6 4 2

Printed and bound in Belgium

Literature has its share of mad or evil scientists. As science took on a leading role in the development of the modern world, so scientists took on a new importance. However, they were often portrayed with suspicion or even hostility, as eccentrics who threatened the established order rather than as benefactors of society. Hergé himself was fascinated by scientists of every kind, repeated the cliché of the demented and dangerous scientist with the manic professor he created for his family-orientated *The Adventures of Jo, Zette and Jocko,* which he began in 1936 in parallel with Tintin at the request of his French publishers. There in *The Secret Ray* readers encounter a sinister and ruthless villain: a white-coated, hunchbacked scientist with a bushy black beard and dark glasses. Eight years later, however, Hergé doffed his hat to science, creating a scientist of genius and charm, Cuthbert Calculus, modelled on a real person, the Swiss physicist Auguste Piccard, who taught at the University of Brussels and whom he would sometimes see striding down the Avenue Louise. Calculus was thoroughly benign – even if he could erupt with an unexpectedly hot temper. He was chivalrous, an admirer of the fair sex, and capable of inventions great and small, whether a Moon rocket or a clothes-brushing machine. For his most sophisticated inventions he would be courted and even kidnapped by foreign powers that saw their strategic value in them. His shark submarine helped in the search for Red Rackham's treasure, and the sale of its patent allowed the purchase of Marlinspike Hall. For *The Adventures of Tintin*, Professor Calculus became an indispensable scientist and a key character.

Michael Farr

A highly eccentric scientist; romantic, visionary, absent-minded... and a little hard of hearing

Professor Calculus

The first appearance of Professor Calculus; frame from *Red Rackham's Treasure*.

THE MOST EXTRAORDINARY FACT about Professor Cuthbert Calculus is that Tintin waited the best part of 15 years to meet him and then, initially at least, neither the reporter nor Captain Haddock wanted anything to do with him.

The first 11 Tintin adventures came and went in a cavalcade of excitement that included a selection of eccentric professors, but no sign of Professor Calculus. It was only in 1944 with the publication of *Red Rackham's Treasure* that his place in *The Adventures of Tintin* was assured. The absurdly deaf, absent-minded inventor of genius was here to stay, if only because his money allowed

Captain Haddock to purchase Marlinspike Hall, his ancestral home, at the end of the adventure.

Greatly to the benefit of the series, Professor Calculus was to play a lesser or greater (notably the Moon adventures and *The Calculus Affair*) role for the remaining 12 adventures. Although his deafness and obstinacy can drive Captain Haddock to distraction, he is an immensely endearing character, not least because of his very human susceptibility to the fair sex.

Facing page: Frames from *The Castafiore Emerald*.

Below: Frames from *Red Rackham's Treasure*.

CALCULUS THE ROMANTIC

He is a romantic in the broadest sense, whether in such grand designs as taking a manned rocket to the Moon and back or, as a horticulturalist, in breeding a rose he names Bianca after the object of his affection, the stately Castafiore: "Dear lady, I beg you to accept these humble roses, the first of a new variety I have created... I have ventured to give them your beautiful name, 'Bianca'!" Her response is effusive: "They are exquisite!... Ex-x-x-quisite! And what perfume! ... Dear Professor, let me embrace you!" Her kiss of gratitude prompts a delighted blush that seems to burn through the page's paper. Calculus is no butterfly and the Milanese Nightingale retains his affection throughout. He is distraught at news of her arrest in *Tintin and the Picaros*: "That poor child!... In prison!... Just imagine!... I'm absolutely shattered!" A few pages on Captain Haddock describes Castafiore to him as "your precious Bianca!" Nevertheless, arriving later at the guerrilla camp, Calculus cannot help being seduced by the unlikely charms – curlers, spectacles and false teeth – of Alcazar's fearsome spouse Peggy. She first harangues her husband, then turns to his companions:

Above: Frame from *Tintin and the Picaros.*

Facing page: Frames from *Red Rackham's Treasure.*

"These guys your friends?... O.K. I warn them: they think they're gonna make the rules around here, they're mighty mistaken!" To which Calculus gives a warm smile and raises his hat: "Thank you gracious lady, for those kind words!... Please believe that we are extremely touched by your generous welcome, and allow me to offer you our most humble respects..." He leans forward and in a most chivalrous manner kisses her hand: "That a weak woman should share the hardships and, let us admit it, the dangers of guerrilla life, commands not only our utmost respect but our profound admiration!... And I speak in all sincerity, dear lady!" When it comes to women, Calculus is an old-fashioned romantic, something of a Don Quixote in search of his Dulcinea. In a series of adventures where there is little time for romance, this provides welcome and delightful relief.

DEAFNESS

Calculus is primarily a comic figure on account of the deafness that leads to a constant stream of misunderstandings. Like many people whose hearing is in decline, the Professor is himself reluctant to admit it, acknowledging only that he may be hard of hearing. Yet when the handicap could impair vital work or, for instance, his own participation in the Moon project, he takes to using an ear trumpet with mixed results, and eventually a hearing aid for the mission itself with a very marked benefit. After its proven success, one wonders why following his return from the Moon he dispenses with the device. The answer is probably vanity and, as far as Hergé was concerned, a reduction in his comic potential.

Left: Frame from *The Castafiore Emerald*.

Facing page: Detail of frame from *Destination Moon*.

Below
Top: Extract from *Destination Moon*.
Bottom: Illustration of old ear trumpets, taken from an engraving in an early 20th century medical dictionary.

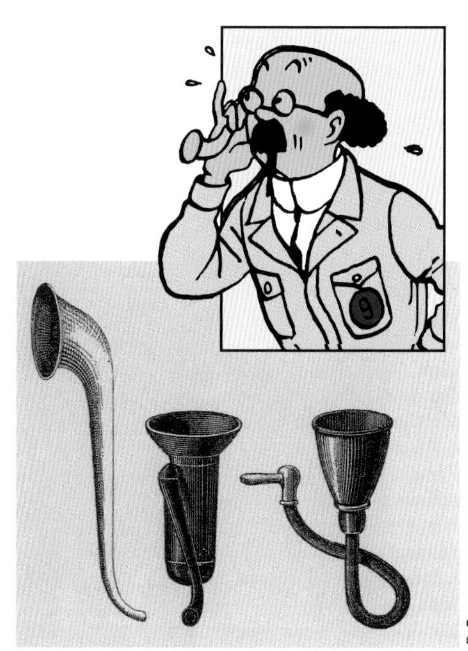

D.R.

The ear trumpet first appears in *Destination Moon* following the arrival of Tintin and Haddock at the Sprodj Research Centre. Calculus whips it out of his top pocket and the reporter remarks: "Ah, you're using an ear trumpet now! But why not a hearing aid – one of those little instruments fitting into the ear? They're almost invisible." To which, the Professor replies: "Oh yes, I know what you mean... But they're meant for deaf people... and I'm only a little hard of hearing in one ear..." Later the Captain notices something different about the Professor. "There you see?... He isn't deaf anymore! He can hear as well as you and me!" Haddock tells Tintin. A small contraption and wire are visibly attached to Calculus's right ear. "In the first place, I never was deaf... Just a little hard of hearing in one ear... But for the Moon journey I need to hear the radio signals perfectly... So that's why I obtained a hearing aid," he explains.

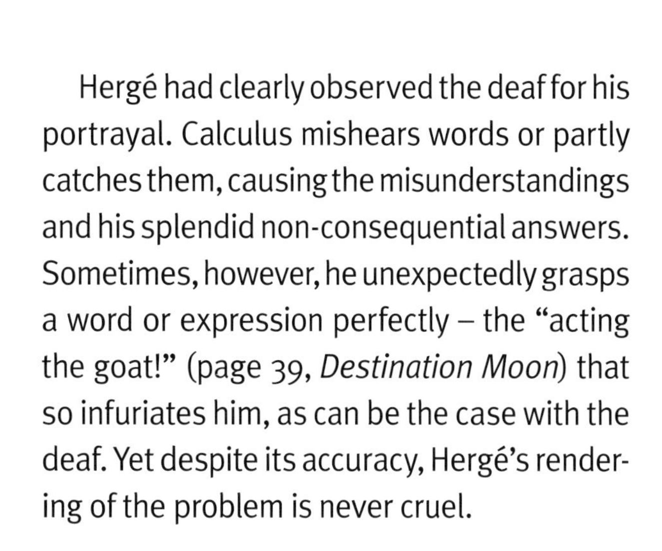

Hergé had clearly observed the deaf for his portrayal. Calculus mishears words or partly catches them, causing the misunderstandings and his splendid non-consequential answers. Sometimes, however, he unexpectedly grasps a word or expression perfectly – the "acting the goat!" (page 39, *Destination Moon*) that so infuriates him, as can be the case with the deaf. Yet despite its accuracy, Hergé's rendering of the problem is never cruel.

CALCULUS'S SPORTING PROWESS

In stark contrast to Calculus's infirmity is his self-confessed athletic prowess, which he takes great pride in detailing in the airport scene of *Flight 714 to Sydney*. When the billionaire aircraft manufacturer Laszlo Carreidas asks hopefully whether he plays the game "Battleships", the Professor mishears: "Battledore? I used to be very good... And not only battledore [a bat used in the game of shuttlecock]. I've been an all-round sportsman in my time... tennis, swimming, rugger, soccer, fencing, skating... I did them all in my young days. Not forgetting the ring, too: wrestling, boxing, and even savate or French boxing... Stars above! They make me laugh nowadays with their judo and karate. Savate! That was real fighting!... Using your feet as well as your fists... I was a champion... unbeatable... just you watch this..." He proceeds to demonstrate with a flying kick and falls flat on his face. He is picked up dazed from the floor: "Perhaps I'm a little out of practise. It'd soon come back if I went into training."

Facing page: Detail from *Flight 714 to Sydney*.

Below: Movements in French boxing, in which feet are used as well as fists, illustrated in the 20th century Larousse, in six volumes, Paris 1928.

HUP!

© AFT

Far left: The billionaire aircraft manufacturer and industrialist Marcel Dassault at the peak of his career, July 1965.

Left: Laszlo Carreidas, detail of frame from *Flight 714 to Sydney*.

Below: Extract from *Flight 714 to Sydney*.

Already in his debut adventure, *Red Rackham's Treasure*, he rows the dinghy carrying Haddock and the buoy to the spot where Tintin has let off the smoke flare. "No, but I was a great sportsman in my youth... And that accounts for the athletic figure I still have... To be quite honest, no... It was mostly walking..." he relates to an otherwise preoccupied Haddock. The Captain clearly knows of the Professor's Olympian aspirations when some pages on in the same adventure, in a display of impatience with Calculus and his pendulum, he snatches the device and hurls it away: "Now your infernal pendulum's gone west, you Olympic athlete, you!"

Above: Frames from *Destination Moon.*

Calculus is not overmodest about either his sporting achievement or his scientific inventions, but traces of his past as an athlete are evident. Note how, his strength fuelled by fury, he lifts with such apparent ease the massively square-shouldered security guard in *Destination Moon* and hangs him up by his collar on the hat and coat rail. Similarly, in another fit of rage, Tintin and Haddock have to save Carreidas from a savage mauling by Calculus in *Flight 714 to Sydney.*

© Getty

Above
Left: Auguste Piccard in May 1952.
Right: Frame from *Tintin in Tibet*.

PICCARD AS MODEL

For Professor Cuthbert Calculus (Tryphon Tournesol in the French original – Tournesol translates as sunflower, while Tryphon was the unusual first name of a carpenter Hergé had come across) Hergé had a very particular model in mind: Auguste Piccard, a remarkable Swiss scientist who held a professorship at the University of Brussels and was a familiar figure in the Belgian capital. Hergé recalled spotting his distinctive, lanky frame striding down the street during the 1930s. Piccard stood out on account of his height (almost six foot six inches – 1.96 metres), which he did not share with Professor Calculus, and his somewhat eccentric, old-fashioned

Right: Frame from *Red Rackham's Treasure.*

Below: Auguste Piccard testing a prototype; January 1, 1940.

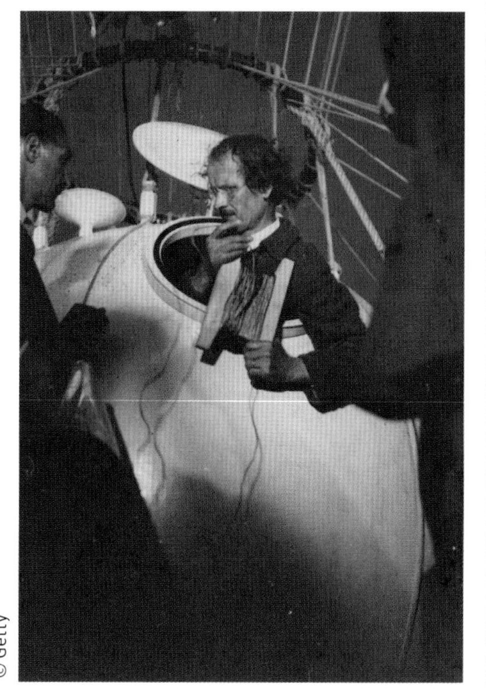

style of dressing – accentuated by an unusually long neck – that was almost identical to Hergé's creation. Unlike Calculus, however, Piccard had perfectly good hearing.

Moreover, like Professor Alembick in *King Ottokar's Sceptre,* Piccard too had a twin brother who was also a distinguished scientist, but in America.

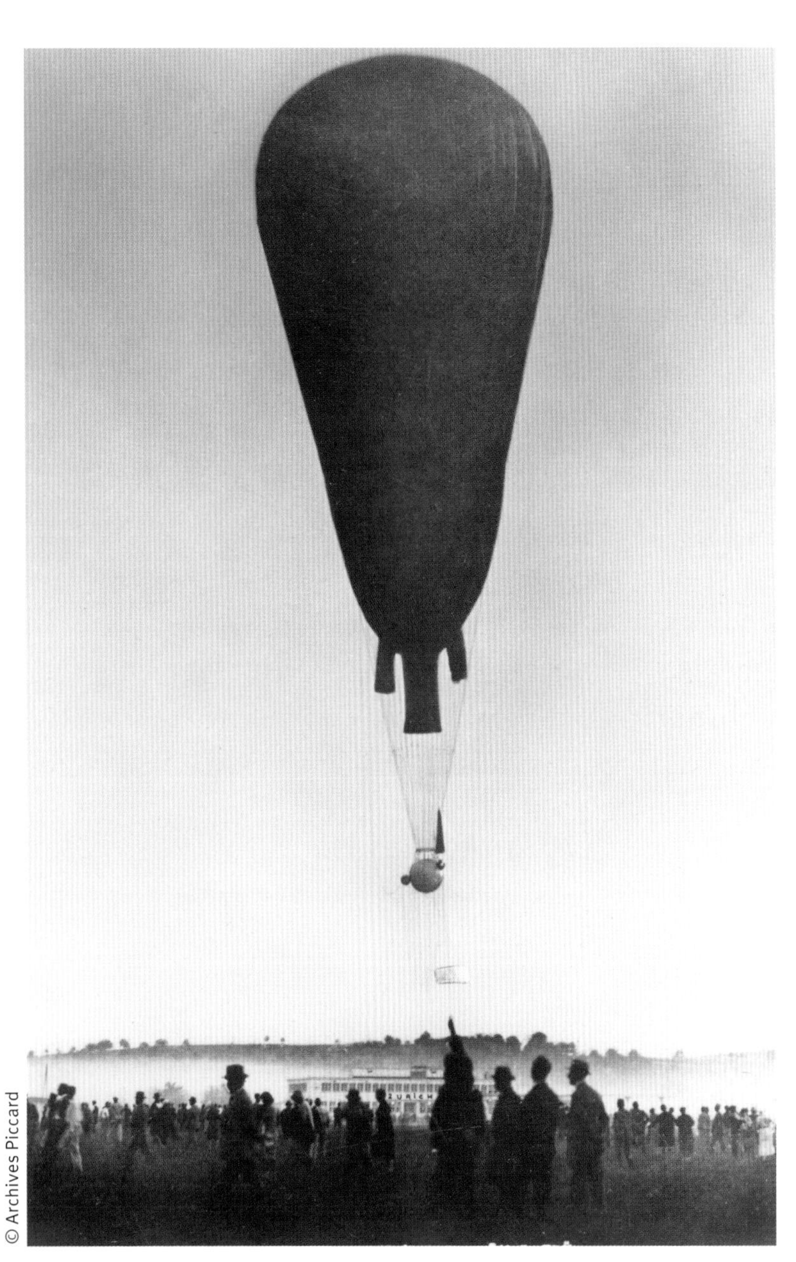

Left: First flight of a stratospheric balloon by Auguste Piccard; May 27, 1931.

Facing page

Left: Frame from *Red Rackham's Treasure.*

Right: Auguste Piccard inspecting a porthole of his bathyscaphe.

Auguste Piccard's chief distinction was before the Second World War to have soared higher into the stratosphere than anyone previously, and afterwards in his bathyscaphe to have plunged deeper into the ocean. Born in Basle in 1884, he became professor of physics at the University of Brussels in 1922, a post he held until 1954. In 1931–32, he made record ascents to 55,000 feet in a balloon of his own design, resulting in important discoveries concerning such stratospheric

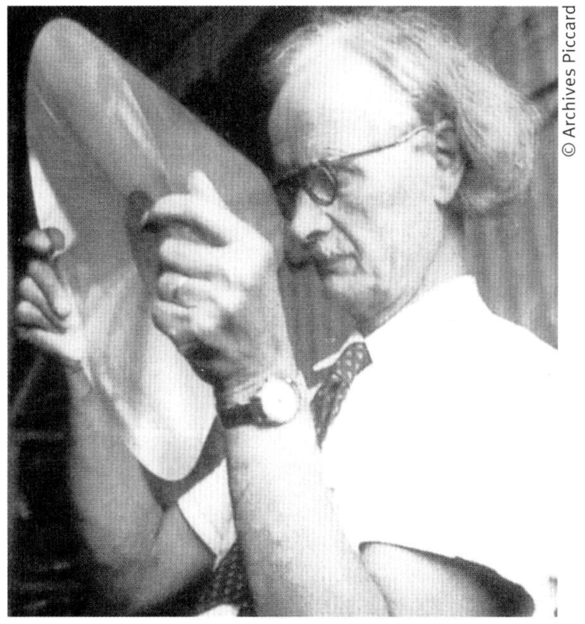

© Archives Piccard

phenomena as cosmic rays. When Professor Calculus is introduced to Bianca Castafiore in *The Castafiore Emerald* and he bends to kiss her hand, popping a collar stud as he does, the prima donna replies: "How enchanting, how absolutely thrilling to meet you: the man who makes all those daring ascents in balloons!" Contemporary photographs show Piccard and a colleague wearing wicker helmets for the record-breaking ascent, as well as a wing-collar and tie! His picture featured regularly in *Le Vingtième Siècle* and other Brussels newspapers that Hergé would see daily. Meanwhile his twin brother Jean, who was professor of aeronautical engineering at the University of Minnesota, made a remarkable balloon ascent together with his wife in Detroit in 1934. Furthermore, demonstrating that ballooning and an appetite for heights could be in the genes, Auguste's grandson Bertrand Piccard became in 1999, together with the Briton Brian Jones, the first to circumnavigate the world non-stop in a balloon. Hergé would have been delighted at such an achievement in the very year that Tintin marked his 70th anniversary.

Left: The bathyscaphe *Trieste* in 1958.

Facing page

Top: Photograph of laboratory in Hergé's archive.

Bottom: Frame from *The Calculus Affair.*

In the post-war years Auguste Piccard built and used bathyscaphes for undersea research, notably the *Trieste,* designed in collaboration with his son Jacques, who in 1960 took it to a depth of 37,800 feet in the Challenger Deep of the Western Pacific. As early as 1953 Auguste Piccard had taken the *Trieste* down to 10,385 feet (3,150 metres). In 1961 Piccard's bathyscaphe *L'Archimède* was launched at Toulon and plunged the following year to a depth of more than 31,350 feet in the Japan Trench. She was built of steel alloy with nickel and molybden chrome, weighed 60 tons and could withstand pressures of 180,000 tons.

In 1962 the outstanding physicist and inventor who inspired Professor Calculus died, leaving his son to carry on his experiments at the bottom of the ocean. His twin brother Jean, who had shared his interest in the stratosphere, died in 1963. Jacques Piccard went on to design a submarine for tourism that could carry 40 passengers and which he named the *Auguste Piccard*, after his father.

CALCULUS THE INVENTOR

It is therefore strangely appropriate that Professor Calculus's entry into *The Adventures of Tintin* comes as a result of his invention of a one-man submarine, which he proposes to Tintin and Haddock as an aid to their search for *Red Rackham's Treasure*. Published in book form in 1944, the adventure thus predates Auguste Piccard's submarine achievements. Similarly Calculus's most outstanding feat, landing the first man on the Moon in 1953, anticipated the American achievement by 16 years! Calculus's rocket is nuclear-powered – considered at the time a viable option – and among the findings credited to Auguste Piccard is Uranium 235. Other inventions of his, apart from the bathyscaphe, include the principal of the pressurised capsule and ultra precise scales, seismograph and galvanometer. He shared Calculus's hunger for

Left: Frame from *Land of Black Gold*.

Below: Three frames from *The Calculus Affair*.

Facing page

Left: An experimental television picture from the 1930s by John Logie Baird.

Top and bottom right: Frames from *The Castafiore Emerald*.

experiment and thirst for invention, though Hergé's Professor included the practical and banal among his list of inventions: a new device for putting bubbles into soda water, a clothes-brushing machine, a collapsible wall-bed, motorised roller-skates and colour television. In *The Calculus Affair* he makes a potentially dangerous breakthrough in the use of ultrasonic sound.

Professor Calculus also has some ability as a chemist – a discipline not shared with

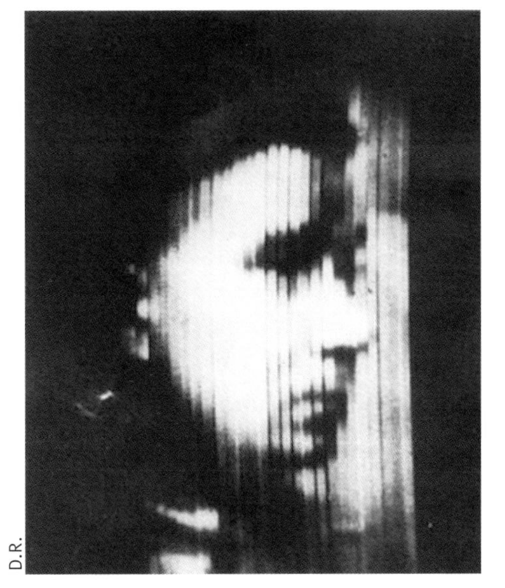

D.R.

Piccard – devising an antidote to Dr Müller's Formula Fourteen in *Land of Black Gold,* though causing extensive damage to Marlinspike in the process, and subsequently, in the final adventures, working on a pill which makes alcohol distasteful (*Tintin and the Picaros*) and then palatable again (*Tintin and Alph-Art*).

SOME NOTABLE INVENTIONS

Red Rackham's Treasure

Red Rackham's Treasure

Red Rackham's Treasure

Land of Black Gold

Tintin and the Picaros

Red Rackham's Treasure

The Calculus Affair

The Red Sea Sharks

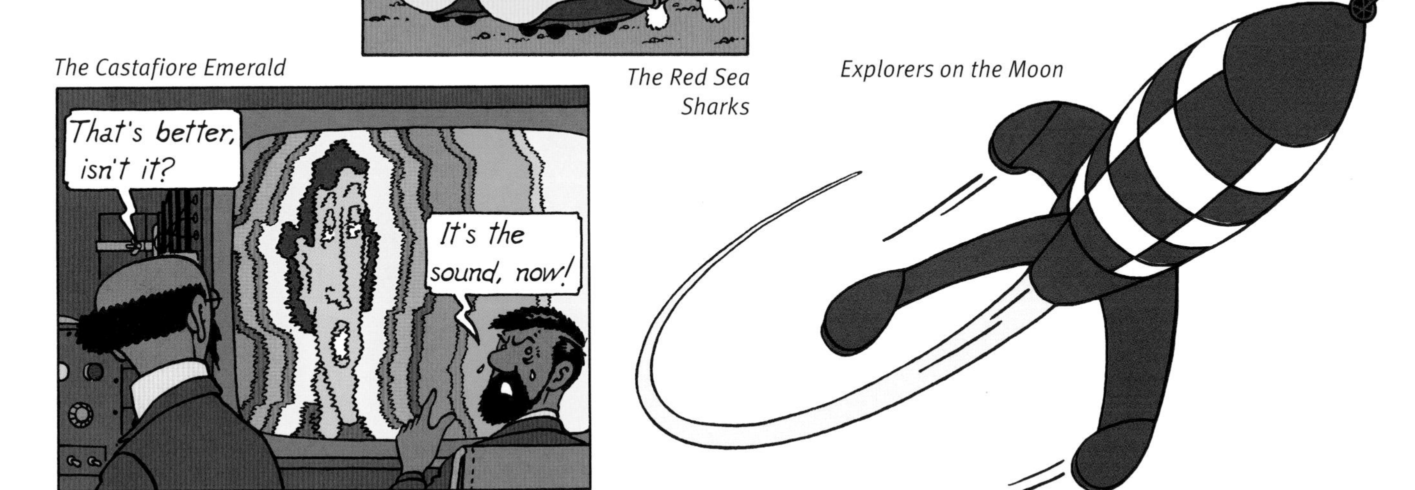

The Castafiore Emerald

Explorers on the Moon

A MOST DISTINCTIVE APPEARANCE

Like Piccard, a highly conservative, old-fashioned appearance – both men would insist on always wearing a tie and had a preference for stiff, starched collars – belied a position at the cutting edge of science. In his interviews with Numa Sadoul, Hergé admitted that Calculus was to take on an importance in the adventures that he did not anticipate when he introduced him in *Red Rackham's Treasure* with his pocket submarine in the form of a shark. "Tournesol [Calculus] and his submarine, were ... above all Professor Auguste Piccard and his bathyscaphe. But Piccard on a reduced scale, because the real professor was very tall. He had an endless neck that soared out of a collar that was far too big. I would bump into him sometimes in the street and he struck me as the very incarnation of a scientist. So I made Tournesol a mini-Piccard, otherwise I would have had to enlarge the frames of the cases!..."

While Piccard had a moustache and spectacles, Hergé gave Calculus a goatee

D.R.

Facing page

Left: Detail of frame from *The Seven Crystal Balls*.

Right: Auguste Piccard dressed in a manner unmistakeably evocative of Professor Calculus.

Below: Detail from *The Castafiore Emerald*.

as well. They dressed in a similar fashion – white shirt, collar and narrow dark tie, black trousers, green jacket and overcoat, hat and indispensable umbrella (which even goes on the Moon mission). Once, in *The Seven Crystal Balls*, we find Calculus wearing a black jacket, which looks particularly smart and well cut. He would sometimes add a buff-coloured waistcoat to his ensemble and, if gardening, a broad-rimmed panama hat. Piccard would often wear a beret and cape and go out with a stick. On the deck of the Sirius in *Red Rackham's Treasure* and again towards the end of *The Calculus Affair*, Calculus sports such a beret.

We do not know about Piccard's night-wear, but Calculus has a preference for nightshirts, as we know from *The Seven Crystal Balls* (plain white) and *Destination Moon* (lilac), though he changes to cream (and later light green) pyjamas in the final completed adventure, *Tintin and the Picaros*, over which he wears a smart dressing gown. He is also shown in an incongruous yellow towelling bathrobe that, absorbed in a book, he forgets to take off in the bath.

Both pages: Frames from *Prisoners of the Sun*.

Although an old-fashioned dresser, Calculus has an unexpected taste for jewellery that leads to trouble in *The Seven Crystal Balls* when he finds and picks up the gold bracelet of Rascar Capac: "Magnificent!... It's obviously made of solid gold... I'll put it on and go indoors wearing it, and see if they notice... Really splendid... And how well it goes with my coat!" Calculus never makes it back to the house and we next find him in Peru in the sequel adventure, *Prisoners of the Sun*, where he is held captive by the Incas for having committed the sacrilege of putting on the sacred bracelet. He is led out by a choir of chanting virgins to join Tintin and Haddock on the sacrificial pyre. Needless to say he is still wearing his starched collar and thin black tie, but on

top he has a colourful, patterned sacrificial robe and an extravagant mitre-like hat with an eagle's head. On the final page his commitment to hats is demonstrated by a bright red Inca wool cap with ear flaps, an incongruous accessory for the long journey home. Calculus is clearly very attached to his familiar green overcoat, identical to one worn by Piccard, often keeping it on indoors, and even, when he is in a drug-induced sleep aboard the Pachacamac, wearing it in bed.

WE ARE NOT INTERESTED IN YOUR MACHINE!

OBSTINACY AND MISUNDERSTANDING

Professor Calculus has all the self-assurance and stubbornness, as well as some of the petulance, of the scientist determined to see his ideas through. This persistence is evident at his first meeting with Tintin and Haddock in *Red Rackham's Treasure* when he will not take no for an answer, even when to counter his deafness Haddock writes it on the wall. He had already dragged Tintin and Haddock against their will to his workshop and showed them the shark submarine prototype before it collapsed under his weight: "No, Professor Calculus, I said your machine won't do for us!" To which he replies astonishingly: "Oh, good!... Well gentlemen, that's agreed. I'll make another smaller one..."

There is a similar misunderstanding in *Destination Moon* when, over a bottle of port, Calculus invites Tintin and Haddock to join him on the mission to the Moon. "Me?... On the Moon!... With you?... Blistering barnacles! Your brain's gone radioactive! On the Moon! You'd just push me around, like that, without a word!... I'll never set foot in your infernal rocket, d'you hear me? Thundering typhoons!... Never!" Without flinching the Professor responds: "Oh, thank you,

Right: *Radiesthésie, Téléradiesthésie et phénomènes hyperphysiques*, a book on dowsing published in Brussels in 1949 that Hergé acquired.

Facing page and below: Extracts from *Red Rackham's Treasure*.

Captain... thank you!... I knew I could count on you." The observant reader will have noticed that listening to Haddock's outburst, Calculus had in a Nelsonian touch picked up the Captain's pipe and held it to his ear instead of his hearing-trumpet.

DOWSING

Another interest of the Professor is dowsing or divining, for which he carries a pendulum and succeeds in irritating Captain Haddock on numerous occasions, but otherwise achieves very little. In *Red Rackham's Treasure* his pendulum is forever directing him westwards to no avail. When he is totally immersed in scientific projects such as the Moon rocket or the ultrasonic experiments of *The Calculus Affair*, this less serious side pursuit is forgotten, though it is taken up by the Thom(p)sons – again without success – in their hunt for the Professor in *Prisoners of the Sun*. The pendulum can be seen dangling out of Calculus's pocket in the hotel scene at the start of *Tintin in Tibet* and he puts it to use once more in *The Castafiore Emerald* and *Flight 714 to Sydney*.

CALCULUS ASSERTS HIMSELF

Hergé's introduction of Calculus in *Red Rackham's Treasure* achieved several objectives that strengthen the narrative so successfully that he could not dispense with him subsequently, even in adventures like *Tintin in Tibet* or *Tintin and Alph-Art,* as we know it, when he just has a minor, walk-on role, or *Land of Black Gold* where he only participates by post at the end.

Firstly, he fulfilled Hergé's desire for an eccentric, absent-minded professor type. The earlier adventures had been punctuated by such professors. The mentally

Both pages: Some other scientists to be found in *The Adventures of Tintin.*

Facing page: Frame from *The Shooting Star.*

unstable Doctor Sarcophagus in *Cigars of the Pharaoh*, the anonymous and wholly distrait professor in *The Broken Ear* (page 6), the chain-smoking Sigillographer, Professor Hector Alembick (a play on the well-known Belgian beer, Lambic, while in English an alembic is an apparatus formerly used in distilling) in *King Ottokar's Sceptre*, Professor Phostle and a gallery of fellow academics in *The Shooting Star*. Professor Fang Hsi-ying in *The Blue Lotus*, "the world authority on madness," is an exception for being portrayed as a wholly serious character without eccentricity.

Post-Calculus and apart from him, Hergé manages furthermore to fill a hospital ward with professors, stricken with a mystery ailment, in *The Seven Crystal Balls* and *Prisoners of the Sun*.

Secondly, the inclusion of Professor Calculus allowed Hergé obvious scope to tackle scientific subjects, best exemplified in the Moon adventures and *The Calculus Affair*. Even at this stage, *The Adventures*

Facing page: Frame from *The Seven Crystal Balls.*

Below: Detail from *The Calculus Affair.*

of Tintin retained some of the pedagogic aims of the early *Petit Vingtième* days, if only on account of the primarily youthful readership. *Tintin* magazine, in which the post-war adventures first appeared, strove to instruct as well as to entertain.

Thirdly, Professor Calculus injects an added, different level of humour through his constant mishearing and misunderstandings, quite different to the slapstick comedy provided by the Thom(p)sons or the irascible buffoonery of Captain Haddock. For this reason and for continuity, once established, Hergé could not drop him. His permanence is demonstrated by the fact that after he helps Haddock buy Marlinspike Hall with money from the patent for his submarine, he moves in with the Captain and they are later joined by Tintin. The three are permanent fixtures, of Marlinspike and of the subsequent adventures.

In the last completed adventure, *Tintin and the Picaros*, it is Professor Calculus who has the final word, as he had in his first adventure 32 years earlier. "Blistering barnacles, I shan't be sorry to be back home at Marlinspike..." says Captain Haddock. "Me too, Captain..." replies Tintin as they fly over the shanty towns of San Theodoros. "Me too, but with a little mustard if you please," Calculus adds, winding up proceedings with an ultimate non sequitur. ■

412

FT
LIFT